HAPPY NEW YEAR

IN

SRI LANKA

BY Christobel Weerasinghe

TO MY GRANDCHILDREN
DIANTHE AND GAVIN

Illustrations

by

DEEPA

of GRANT, KENYON AND ECKHARDT LTD.

edited by

PAULINE INNIS

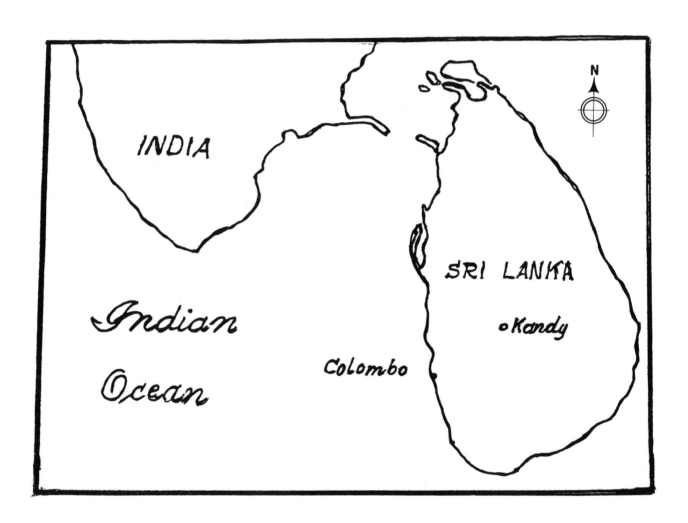

Gavin and his sister Dianthe are visiting their grandmother in Sri Lanka for the new year.

Sri Lanka is a tropical island at the tip of India. It used to be called Ceylon.

If you look at the map you will see where Sri Lanka is.

New Year's Day marks the bringing in of the harvest and the beginning of Spring.

Because it is a tropical island, Sri Lanka does not have four seasons. Instead there are two rainy seasons or monsoons. The heavy rainfall during the monsoon seasons make it possible to grow the rice or paddy crops which are the main food of the people. Also to grow the Ceylon tea for export. The paddy fields and tea plantations are a familiar part of the landscape where you go in Sri Lanka.

Dianthe and Gavin like the New Year Festival best of all because it is very special and they have lots of fun and always go to their grandmother's house to see the rest of their relatives. The New Year is the time when families get together. Everyone tries to get home for the New Year just as Americans do for Thanksgiving.

Dyantha and Gavin's grandmother always tells them stories about the things she did on New Year's Day when she was little. Most of the things are the same, but some of the old customs have been changed.

Lighting the fire on the hearth and cooking the first meal of the New Year is the most important moment.

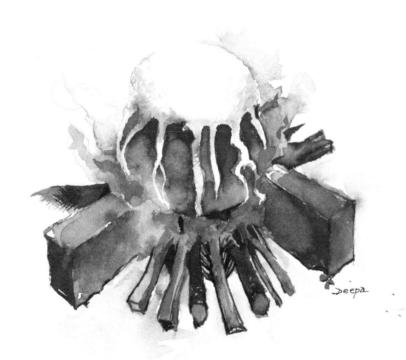

The right time for lighting the fire is decided by the astrologers who also announce the auspicious times for other activities during the Festival.

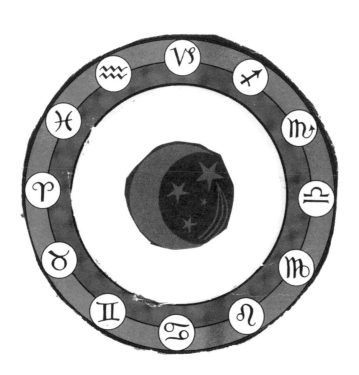

From early times it has been customary for the people of Sri Lanka to kneel and with clasped hands pay homage to their elders on New Year's Day. Also, it is customary to offer betel leaves to each other as a sign of goodwill.

Betel Leaves

Everyone has new clothes for the New Year and these are made in the color the astrologers have decided is auspicious. The auspicious color depends on the day of the week New Year's Day falls on. Each day has its own planet and each planet has its own color. For instance, Saturday is the planet Saturn's day and its color is red.

Dyanthe and Gavin like to help lay the New Year's table. This is a time honored ceremony and must be done a certain way. The traditional brass lamp with 7 cloth wicks burning brightly, is placed in the center of the table. Beside it is a traditional dish of milk rice.

Sweetmeats, candies, cookies and special dishes of many kinds are all carefully prepared for the family meal and placed on the table. Fruits such as plantains, mangoes and pineapples are arranged on leaves lending color and freshness. Then, at last, the whole family sit together at the table and enjoy the feast.

Deepa

Afterwards the family and domestic helpers exchange gifts. Then it is time for religious services.

The sound of the temple bells ringing reminds people that it is time to go and make their devotions and offerings. The temple is very old and beautiful. Dyanthe and Gavin like to go there and they like to hear the bells which ring all through New Year's week to signal the different events.

TEMPLE

ANURADHAPURA

In the rural areas people travel to the temples in two wheeled carts pulled by bullocks.

The children think it is very exciting to ride in the carts dressed in their new clothes of the special New Year color.

They hope

they will see

an elephant

or a

crocodile

on the way.

Most often

it is a brightly colored bird

or a deer they will see

hiding among the trees.

Sri Lanka has very many birds, animals and flowers everywhere. In the year 3 B.C. the King of Sri Lanka made an order to start the first Wildlife Park in the whole world.

If you go to Mihintale you can visit it. The Park is now over two thousand years old.

The New Year Fesitval lasts for a week and all kinds of games take place. Children play on swings and their mothers and big sisters make music on a large drum called a rabana.

A rabana is made of cowhide stretched across a circular base. Small ones are about ten inches across and the large ones are thirty inches or more in diameter.

Four or five women sit around the drum and play on it with their hands.

The New Year Festival is specially joyful because everybody celebrates it. The Singhala Bhuddists, the Tamil Hindus and Christians all join in.

Many of the traditions which took place during the days of the Kandian kings have been forgotten, but many stay the same. The New Year has deep importance for Sri Lankans because the customs have endured for 2,500 years.

One day Gavin and Dianthe went with their grandmother to the ocean. They went to a place called Bentota which is south of Columbo where their Grandmother lives.

The sands are soft and golden and the sea is blue and calm. Lots of palm trees make shady places if the sun gets too hot.

Dianthe and Gavin met some little friends and they all went swimming together. Then they went looking for shells and found some very pretty ones to take home.

There were some fishermen casting their nets out into the sea. Many people make a living fishing. There are a lot of different kinds of fish in the sea around Sri Lanka.

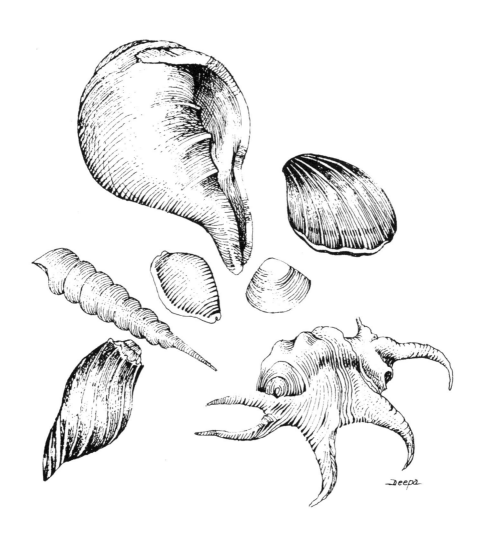

Later, they went to the open air theatre and saw the dancers.
Some were wearing masks which made them look like devils.

Another day they all went to Kandy which is a very old city. It was the home of the ancient Sinhala Kings.

Every year there is a great Festival in Kandy. It is called the Festival of the August Moon.

It ends with a great procession in honor of the Sacred Tooth Relic of Buddha. This procession winds through the streets in the moonlight. People from all over the world come for this event.

It is an amazing sight. Dancers leap and whirl among the stately chiefs riding on the richly decorated elephants. Music is made by drummers, oboe players and singers.

"I will take you to see it one day," their grandmother promised Dianthe and Gavin.

ABOUT THE AUTHOR.

Christobel Weerasinghe lives in Sri Lanka but she knows the United States very well as her husband was Ambassador here for a number of years.

Mrs Weerasinghe is well known as a lecturer on Sri Lanka in the United States and she teaches nursery rhymes and dance steps to children in two villages in Sri Lanka. She has made a number of records of the folk songs and dances of other lands.